For William Caspar Newell – MM

For Jasmine, with love – AC

First published 2007 by Macmillan Children's Books
a division of Macmillan Publishers Limited
20 New Wharf Road, London N1 9RR
Basingstoke and Oxford
Associated companies throughout the world
www.panmacmillan.com

ISBN: 978-1-4050-5401-0 (HB)
ISBN: 978-0-230-01464-0 (PB)

Text copyright © Miriam Moss 2007
Illustrations copyright © Anna Currey 2007
Moral rights asserted.

1 3 5 7 9 8 6 4 2

A CIP catalogue record for this book is available from the British Library.

Printed in Belgium by Proost

Bedtime, Billy Bear!

MIRIAM MOSS

Illustrated by ANNA CURREY

MACMILLAN CHILDREN'S BOOKS

When Billy and Rabbit splashed in from the garden,
Mum and her friend Lucy were having a cup of tea.

"Oh, just look at you, Billy!" cried Mum.

"You're completely covered in mud!"

Billy looked down at his trousers.

"Yes," he said, "and look! So is Rabbit!"

"I think it's time for a bath," said Mum.

Mum washed Billy,
and Billy washed Rabbit.

"Billy," said Mum, "have you remembered that Lucy is looking after you tonight while I go to my pottery class?"

"Yes, I remembered," said Billy,

"but Rabbit forgot."

Mum helped Billy into his pyjamas.
"Billy," she smiled, "are you looking where
you're putting your feet?"

"I was," said Billy, "but I've lost Rabbit. Where is she?"

"Look, she's over there," said Mum, "drying out after her bath.
She can carry on drying out downstairs while you
have your snack."

When he got downstairs, Billy showed Lucy his new pyjamas.
"Oh, they're lovely, Billy," said Lucy.
"Yes, Rabbit chose them," said Billy.

After his snack, Billy went to find Rabbit.
She was lovely and warm and dry.

Billy yawned.

"Rabbit's very tired, you know," he said.

"Yes," said Mum, "I can see that. Come on, up we go!"

Mum helped Billy brush his teeth.

"You have to look this way, Billy," she said.

"I can't," said Billy. "Rabbit's fidgeting.

I think something's bothering her."

"What could that be?" said Mum.

"She wants to come to pottery with you," said Billy.

"I'm afraid it's far too late for a young rabbit to be out," said Mum. "But I could make something for her."

Mum read Billy a story and then kissed him goodnight.
"You've forgotten to sing our song," said Billy.

"I've got to go to pottery now," said Mum.
"But here's Lucy. She's going to sing with you tonight."
Mum tucked Billy in.
"Goodnight, Billy. Sleep tight!" she said.

"Lucy, can we sing a noisy song?" Billy asked.

"Of course we can," smiled Lucy.

After the noisy song she sang a soft, going-to-sleep song.

Then she kissed Billy and went downstairs.

Silence poured into Billy's room.

"Lucy!" shouted Billy.
"You forgot to kiss Rabbit."

Lucy came back. She kissed Rabbit
and then kissed Billy again.
"Now close your eyes and go to sleep,"
she said, and left.

Billy closed his eyes,
but he just couldn't sleep.

He climbed out of bed and sat on the stairs.

"What are you doing, Billy?" asked Lucy.
"Rabbit's worried because there's a funny noise
in my room," he said.

Lucy came back upstairs to listen to the noise.
"That's just the wind blowing in the chimney!" said Lucy.
"Oh," said Billy.
Lucy tucked him back into bed.

Billy peered over his duvet into the corner of the room
where all the dark collected. He didn't like it one bit.

He grabbed Rabbit, jumped out of bed
and hurried downstairs.

"Rabbit can't get to sleep," began Billy.
"Billy," said Lucy, "if Rabbit is going to be naughty and keep you awake,
I'm afraid she's going to have to sleep somewhere else."

Billy's eyes grew wide.
"I don't think she'll like that," he said.

"Well then you'd better tell her to behave."
Billy's eyes filled with tears.

Lucy lifted Billy gently on to her knee.
"What's the matter, Billy?" she asked.
"It's the dark," said Billy. "Mum won't be able
to find her way home in all the dark."

Lucy took Billy over to the window.

"Look how the moon and stars light up the garden," she said.

"And look at the street lights. Mum will definitely be able to find her way home. She always does, doesn't she?"

Billy nodded.

"Shall we go upstairs now?" asked Lucy.
"We don't want Mum to come back and find you still up, do we?"
"No," sighed Billy, closing his eyes.

Slowly, Lucy carried Billy back upstairs.

And by the time Mum got home
with the pottery present,

Billy was fast asleep – at last!